Felicia's Family Divorces

THIS CHILDREN'S CONCEPT BOOK BELONGS TO:

_____

Janice Krupic, M.S., & SueAnne Magyar-Hill, Psy.D.

ILLUSTRATED BY: BRIAN MCKISSICK

Children's Concept Publishing, Novi, Michigan

*To Morgan...my sweetpea, and
to my parents, Michael and Margaret, for their ongoing support — J.K.*

To my husband and children for always supporting and believing in my visions. — S.M-H.

Text copyright © 2004 by Janice Krupic and SueAnne Magyar-Hill
Illustrations copyright © 2004 by Brian McKissick
First edition 2004

Felicia Series
An Imprint of Children's Concept Publishing
P.O. Box 954
Novi, MI 48376-0954
www.childrensconcept.org

Editing by Gerri Allen and Jo Ellen Roe
Book design by Buffington & Associates
Author photos by Theresa Kuehn
Printed and bound in the United States of America by McNaughton & Gunn, Inc.

Library of Congress Cataloging-in-Publication Data
Krupic, Janice—Magyar-Hill, SueAnne

Felicia's Family Divorces / Janice Krupic/SueAnne Magyar-Hill ; illustrations by Brian McKissick - 1st ed.
p. cm.

Summary: Felicia Drummond sorts through the many emotions over her parents divorce until she learns what matters most is to have the love and attention of both parents.

ISBN 0-9745219-0-6

(1. Divorce - Fiction; 2. Family Life - Fiction; 3. Self-acceptance - Fiction; 4. Parenting - Fiction)
I. Krupic, Janice; Magyar-Hill, SueAnne; II. McKissick, Brian; III. Title

2003112948

TO CHILDREN
(AND PARENTS)
OF DIVORCED FAMILIES

It doesn't matter whether you have
One parent, two, three or four.
What matters is that you receive the love
You deserve, plus more.

On days when you're feeling
Lonely and blue,
There seems to be no good reason
Why divorce has happened to you.

Further, it's likely you may not
Understand today,
Why all this turmoil and confusion
Has come your way.

So although your family has been through a lot,
Someday you will see
What a special gift of caring you have
That you'll be able to give to others in need.

J.K.

FOR USE BY
HEALTH/FAMILY SYSTEM
PROFESSIONALS

This interactive book is a tool for health/family system professionals to use with children up to ten years old. Felicia's Family Divorces takes seven-year-old Felicia through many of the emotions that children experience during divorce.

Each chapter concludes with an interactive component that you can use to encourage a dialogue between you and your client. The format also provides a way for your client to express feelings he or she may have that are similar to the feelings the characters in the story have. If the client does identify with Felicia, for example, you may be able to better understand his or her point of view without crossing an uncomfortable boundary your client may not be ready to cross.

Felicia's Family Divorces also lends itself to focusing on individual chapters. Focusing narrowly in this way may enable you to elicit information from the client that will help you understand the stage of grief-loss the client is in with regard to the divorce.

We hope you will find this book to be a useful tool in helping your clients gain understanding and adjust in a healthy way to the changes that are taking place in their families.

Janice Krupic, M.S., & SueAnne Magyar-Hill, Psy.D.

FOR USE BY PARENTS

Your children's feelings—and your own—about your divorce will be many. It is normal for your child to be angry one day, sad the next, and excited to see the absent parent on still another. We hope that Felicia's Family Divorces will be helpful to your child or children as they learn to accept the conflicting feelings they and the rest of the family will surely experience.

This book incorporates both an interactive piece and a journaling component at the end of each chapter to assist you in making it safe for your children to express confusion, pain, anger, and sadness. Additionally, you can use this book at different stages of the healing process, depending on where your children are emotionally, as their thoughts and feelings may change over time. Again, such change in emotions is a very normal part of healing from grief and loss that you and your children may experience.

Lastly, no matter what emotions you and your children are experiencing, please remember to constantly remind your children that you love them and always will.

We hope that you will find Felicia's Family Divorces a useful tool in assisting your children and your entire family through what can be a very difficult time. You may find talking with a health/family system professional to be helpful as well.

Janice Krupic, M.S., & SueAnne Magyar-Hill, Psy.D.

TABLE OF CONTENTS

1

Felicia Gets Bad News

That Friday, the Maple Hills school bus stopped at the intersection of Acorn and Oak Streets as it did every afternoon at 3:00. Felicia Drummond, a spunky, seven-and-a-half-year-old, was usually the last one off the bus. Today, though, she and her best friend, Mikala, sat on the edge of the front-row seat.

"I can hardly wait to ask my mom," Felicia told Mikala. "I'm sure she'll let me spend the night."

"I hope so," said Mikala, as the bus pulled away. "Call me and let me know as soon as you find out."

Felicia skipped to the end of her driveway. Suddenly, she noticed that both her mom's car and her dad's car were there. "Where is Sara?" she wondered. "Why are Mom and Dad here?"

Usually Sara watched over Felicia and her two-year-old brother Tyler in the afternoons until her parents got home from work. Dylan, Felicia's older brother, claimed he was too old for a babysitter. "Give me a break," he would complain. "I'm thirteen years old. None of my friends have babysitters." On this sunny early autumn afternoon, it seemed strange that Sara wasn't there.

Felicia knew something was wrong. "Uh-oh," she said to herself. "I hope Gran's okay. And Shilo—please, let Shilo be okay, too. He's such a good dog."

Felicia entered the kitchen through the back door. As she took her backpack off, she looked up and saw her Mom, her Dad, and Dylan sitting at the kitchen table. Tyler was sleeping. "Why is everybody home? Where's Sara? What's wrong?" she asked.

"Felicia, honey, why don't you sit down," her mom said.

Felicia's heart sank, but she sat down. Her guesses about what was wrong weren't even close... the news was much worse.

Her dad spoke. "Kids, you know Mom and I have been arguing a lot lately. Neither one of us is very happy, and well, we've decided to get a divorce. We think it will be best for everyone that we not live together anymore."

Dylan muttered, "Yeah, that figures," and took off on his bike.

Felicia broke into tears and ran upstairs to her room. She threw herself on the bed and lay there, sobbing. She could hear her parents quarreling in the kitchen below. Suddenly the front door slammed.

Felicia ran to the window and watched her dad throw a suitcase in the car and drive away. She could hear her mom crying, but she felt too sad to comfort her. "Dad's gone," she whispered. She took Sam, her favorite stuffed animal, out of the hammock in the corner of her room and hugged him fiercely.

"Maybe he'll come back," she said. "Maybe he'll change his mind and come home."

It was a quiet night at the dinner table. No one except Tyler, who gibbered away in his own language, felt like talking. Mom, her eyes swollen and red, picked at her food. Dylan sat silently in front of the television. Felicia wasn't hungry, either. She ate a bite or two and then laid her fork down. She even forgot about watching her favorite TV show, "Allie and Max."

Soon, though it was only seven o'clock, she went to her room and started getting ready for bed. Dressed in her pajamas, she sat and hugged Sam some more and thought sadly about her family.

Suddenly she remembered she had forgotten to call Mikala, or even to ask about spending the night. "I don't want to call her," she thought. "I don't want to have to tell her about Mom and Dad."

Later in the evening, Felicia's mom knocked on the bedroom door and said, "Can I come in? It's time for me to tuck you in."

Felicia looked at her mom. She said, "Mom, does this mean that we will never see Dad again?"

"Oh, honey, of course not. Dad and I have to work some things out, but he'll be moving into a new house, and you'll be able to spend time with him and me."

"Did I do something wrong? Is that why you and Dad are getting divorced?"

Felicia's mom took a deep breath. A tear ran down her cheek as she said, "Sweetpea, nothing that you or Dylan or Tyler has done is causing Dad and me to get a divorce. We will always care for each other and for you, but we don't need to live together anymore. We fight too much, and there are just some grownup things we can't agree on. Things will be a lot more peaceful with us living apart. I know it seems awful now, but things will get better. I promise."

"Will Dad come back and get some more things?" asked Felicia.

"Yes, Dad will need to have some furniture to put in his new house," said Mom. "He and I will be talking about all that and deciding what will go with him and what will stay here. That way, when you go spend time with him, some of the furniture will be the same."

Felicia threw her arms around her mother's neck, and the two of them sat and cried together for a few minutes. Then her mother whispered in her ear:

"Sometimes moms and dads grow apart,
But always remember
We will both always love you with all our heart."

Then her mom tucked Felicia into bed, kissed her goodnight, and turned out the light. Felicia still felt very sad, but talking with Mom had made her feel just a little bit better.

My Thoughts

What do you think Felicia would say to her dad, if he were tucking her into bed?
What do you think Dylan was thinking about when he went to bed?
Where do you think Felicia's dad went? How do you think he feels?
What do you think Mikala will say when she finds out Felicia's parents are divorcing?

My Space

Draw or write how you would feel if you were Felicia or Dylan.

Can It Be Real?

Felicia and her dad were usually the first ones up on Saturdays. Dad liked the quiet time to read the paper before he took Felicia to her ice skating lessons. Since she was four, Felicia had dreamed of becoming a famous skater. Going to lessons with Dad was one of her favorite times. Sometimes he took her to get a bagel and then sat and watched as she twirled and spun across the ice.

This Saturday was different, though. When Felicia woke up, she felt good for a moment—and then she remembered. Dad was gone.

She got out of bed and slowly wandered downstairs. Felicia felt sad when she got to the kitchen and saw her dad's empty chair. "It's true," she thought. "He's really gone. Now who will take me to ice skating lessons?" A tear ran down her cheek.

When her mom came down for breakfast, she acted as though nothing was different. "Felicia, why aren't you dressed? Your skating practice starts in less than an hour."

"I don't want to skate this morning," said Felicia. "Besides, Dad isn't here to take me."

Felicia's mom was usually firm about making the kids follow through with the commitments they made. But this morning, she was more tolerant than usual. "I was going to take you," she said. "But maybe we could go have some breakfast and then go shopping for your recital outfit. How does that sound? You know, your big day will be here before you know it."

"Okay, I guess," said Felicia. Although she didn't really want to go shopping, either, maybe it would make Mom a little happier.

When they got into the car, Felicia began to tease her baby brother. She handed him a toy he wanted, and then at the last moment, snatched it away. "Got it," she said, and then stuck it out to Tyler once more.

"Felicia, don't be mean," said her mother.

When they got to the mall, Felicia's mom put Tyler in a stroller, and the three of them walked inside. They went from store to store, looking for just the right outfit for Felicia. "I don't like this one," Felicia said, "it's too frilly."

"I don't like this one either," she said. "The headband looks dorky."

"And, this one is the ugliest thing I've ever seen," whined Felicia. She knew she was being horrible, but she couldn't help herself. She felt all grumpy and out of sorts. She was supposed to be skating this morning, with Dad watching her proudly from the side of the ice rink. Instead, here she was trying on clothes she didn't even like.

Finally, Mom lost her temper. She snapped, "Felicia, there's no pleasing you this morning. I am just going to get this one right here. Come on!" She picked it up and grabbed Felicia's arm.

At the register, Felicia glared at her mom. "I hate that outfit, Mom," she said. "But you go on and get it. You always do what you want to do anyway—just like you made Dad leave!" Felicia burst into tears.

Felicia's mom ignored her daughter's outburst as best she could. She paid the cashier and quickly maneuvered Felicia, Tyler's stroller and the shopping bags out of the mall and into the car. The drive home was silent, and anger filled up the space between Felicia and her mom.

Later that evening, after they had each spent some time alone, Felicia's mom came to her room. "It's important that you know that Dad and I decided together to get a divorce. I feel sad and angry, too. I know we are all hurting right now," she said. "I'm so sorry for how you and Dylan are feeling. I know our family is changing, and right now, it seems awful. But I do think things will get better. And even though Dad doesn't live here anymore, you will have a home with him, he will always be a part of your life."

Felicia's mom held her tightly and whispered in her ear:

"Sometimes we laugh, sometimes we cry.
Sometimes we hurt inside and don't know why.
But always remember when you're feeling blue
That Mom and Dad will always love you."

My Thoughts

Why do you think Felicia did not want to go skating?
Why do you think Felicia was so crabby while shopping?
What do you think Dylan did while everyone else was shopping?
How do you think Felicia's mom felt at the end of the day?

My Space

Draw or write what you think would make Felicia feel better.

3

Moving Out

During the following week, Felicia got to see her dad quite a bit. Every afternoon when she came home from school, he was there. He and her mom were talking a lot, and it didn't seem as if they were arguing as much as they had.

Felicia began to hope that Dad would come back. "Hey, Dad," she said one afternoon. "When are you moving back in here with us?"

"I'm not, honey," said Dad. "I have a new house over on Maple Street. It's not too far from here. You'll be able to spend time with me as well as your Mom and not have to change schools."

"Will you be moving furniture over there?" asked Felicia, feeling sad all over again.

"Yes, that's what your mom and I have been talking about," he said. "I need a bed to sleep in, and I thought I'd take the one in the guest bedroom for now. And soon I want you to help me shop for beds for you and Dylan and Tyler to sleep in when you spend time with me. How would that be?"

"Yea, Dad, I'll go shopping with you. What else are you taking?"

"I'll take my chair I sit in when I watch TV, and I'll take the old sofa and the table and chairs from downstairs. And of course, I have to get the rest of my clothes and my books."

"When are you going to do all this?" asked Felicia dully, fighting back tears.

"Saturday," said Dad. "I'll bring a truck and load everything up. I could use a little help then, too. Maybe you and Dylan can be available." He reached out and patted Tyler on the head. "I don't think this guy will be much help, though."

"Dad, I don't want you to go. You're mean to ask me to help you move out!" cried Felicia, bursting into tears. She ran to her room and threw herself on the bed.

A few minutes later, her dad knocked on the door. "Can I come in, Felicia?"

"Yes," said Felicia, sitting up.

Dad came over and sat beside Felicia. "I know how hard this is, honey," he said, as he drew Felicia to him and gave her a hug. "Like your mom said, we all feel sad right now. But always remember, no matter what happens, I will always love you and take care of you. I'll always be your dad."

Felicia nuzzled up to her dad. She still felt horribly sad, but somewhat comforted, too.

That Saturday, when Felicia got home from ice skating lessons, Dad was there with a moving truck. The truck was backed up to the front porch, and he and a friend of his were just putting the sofa from the basement into the back of it.

When he saw her, Dad said, "Hi, Sweetpea. How did your lesson go?"

"It was fine, Dad," said Felicia. "But I missed you being there."

"I promise I'll take you next weekend, Felicia," said Dad. We'll make a morning out of it. Dylan can come along, and then the three of us can go out to lunch. How will that be?"

"That will be fine, Dad," said Felicia, though she felt anything but happy. "What do you need me to do to help?"

"There are some boxes on the steps," said Dad. "Maybe you could bring the lightest ones and put them in the truck."

Felicia helped lift the boxes that weren't too heavy, and soon the truck was all packed up. As Dad got in and drove away, Felicia waved. When the truck turned the corner, she sat on the front porch and cried and cried. "He's really gone now," she thought. "And he's not coming back."

My Thoughts

Why do you think Felicia thought her dad was mean to ask her to help him move?
Why do you think Dylan would not help his dad?
How do you think Felicia's mom felt when her husband was moving his things out?
How could Felicia help herself feel better?

_____

_____

_____

_____

_____

_____

_____

_____

_____

_____

_____

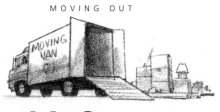

My Space

Draw or write how you would feel if you were Felicia or Dylan.

4

Life With Two Homes

The following Saturday, the weekend before Halloween, Felicia was still feeling all mixed up and unhappy inside. Even the thought of going to her skating lesson with Dad wasn't making her feel good. Felicia sat in her room and listened to her mother arguing with Dylan.

"Dylan, hurry up and get your stuff. You have had all morning to get ready. It's ridiculous to make your dad wait for you."

Dylan mouthed back, "Why does my weekend have to be ruined because you and Dad decided to live in different places? I have plans with my friends. It figures—I have to do what everyone else wants me to do. No one cares what I want!"

"Dylan, of course we care what you want!" said Mom. "But your dad wants to spend time with you too!"

When Dad knocked at the door, Dylan opened it. "Why do I have to go with you to the ice skating rink?" he said. "Why can't I just stay here and go out with my friends?"

"Since I will not get to see you everyday," said Dad, "I want us to spend time together."

"Yeah, right," muttered Dylan. "We're just one big happy family, aren't we?"

Felicia came into the room holding the new bag that Grandma bought for her. She hugged her dad, but inside, she felt miserable. She handed the bag to Dad, who went to put it in the car. Then she gave her mom and Tyler a kiss.

"Don't worry, honey," said her mom. "Dylan is having a hard time, too. You guys have a good time with your dad. And remember that I love you very much."

Felicia walked out the door. Dylan followed her and slammed it shut.

"Maybe we'll have a good time, Dylan," said Felicia. "I'm glad you're going to my skating lessons with me."

Dad had the whole weekend planned for them. He promised that after they were done at the ice rink, they could go pick pumpkins. After that, they could go to "Riley's Rain Forest"—the coolest restaurant in town.

Felicia squealed with excitement. Dylan, however, was a different story. "Give me a break. We have to sit through this stupid skating, pick out stupid pumpkins and go to a place where there are a lot of stupid people! Why can't you just let me stay home?" he yelled.

"Dylan, I am doing the best I can," said Dad, "and I could surely use your help. I love you, son. I know this is hard for you. But you need to understand that your mom and I are doing what we think will be best for all of us in the long run."

The morning went a little better after that. Felicia enjoyed her lessons. Most of all she enjoyed having Dad and Dylan watching her. They got to ride through a pumpkin patch on an old truck, too, and that was fun. They even picked out a couple of cool-looking pumpkins, and Felicia found herself looking forward to carving them in the afternoon. But lunch at Riley's Rain Forest didn't go so well.

First, they had to wait over an hour to get a seat. Then, Felicia spilled her pop all over the table and down her new 'Tommy Walker' shirt her dad had just bought. While Dad went to get extra napkins to clean up the mess, Felicia said to Dylan, "Maybe we can talk Dad into making up with Mom."

"Get real," responded Dylan. "Mom and Dad aren't getting back together. When are you going to get that through your head?"

Dad walked up just in time to hear Felicia say, "Why are you always so mean?"

"Stop this nonsense right now," he said. "I try to show you kids a good time and all you do is argue!"

They ate their meal quickly. Both Dad and Dylan were angry and silent, but Felicia just felt like crying. She tried to hide the tears that trickled down her face, but she couldn't. "What will happen if Dad gets mad at me?" she wondered. "Will he stop spending time with me? Besides, if he's not mad at Mom anymore, why can't he just come home?"

On the way out to the car, Dad pulled Felicia over to him for a quick hug. "It'll be all right, Sweetpea," he said. "All this will get better soon."

"Will you still be coming to my recital, Dad?" asked Felicia.

"Honey, I would never miss such an important day," he promised.

Felicia was sad that Dylan was so unhappy and angry, but she was beginning to feel a little better. The rest of the day went pretty well. Even Dylan had fun carving a horrible-looking face in his pumpkin. When Dad took the kids home, Mom had cooked their favorite meal—spaghetti.

"Hi, kids," she said. "I missed you guys. It sure is nice to have you home."

"I'm glad to be home, too," said Felicia. And she realized that the noise Tyler was making banging the pots and pans together was almost comforting. It had been nice to be with Dad, but it was nice to be home with her Mom and Shilo.

When Felicia's mom tucked her into bed that night, she lay down beside her and gave her extra hugs. Felicia felt happy just to be with her mom, and she knew Mom liked the hugs, too. Quietly her mom sang to her:

"Good night, my Sweetpea,
Remember, there will always be lots of special
times to share.
Just you and me.
I love you with all my heart
Even though your dad and I must part.
Remember, all of us will always be there for you.
Tyler, Dylan, your dad and me.
Good night, and pleasant dreams, my Sweetpea."

My Thoughts

Why do you think Dylan carved an angry pumpkin?
What do you think Dylan's dad could have said to make him feel better?
Why do you think Felicia keeps asking if her mom and dad are getting back together?
What do you think Felicia's mom is doing this weekend?

My Space

Draw or write what you think Dylan or Felicia's pumpkin looked like.

5

We Are Not Alone

Several weeks passed. Felicia and Dylan began to look forward to seeing their dad, but they also looked forward to the weekends they got to stay at home and play with their friends. Felicia was especially excited about the upcoming weekend, because Mom had promised that her friend, Mikala, could spend the night. It was the first time since Dad had moved out.

"She's not coming over, is she?" said Dylan disgustedly.

"Mom said she could, and anyway, why don't you just mind your own business!" retorted Felicia.

"It figures. Anytime I ask Mom if I can have friends spend the night or if I can go over to my friend's house, she comes up with excuses as to why I can't," said Dylan.

Felicia's mom heard the bickering. She entered the kitchen. "You guys remember that Tyler is asleep," she said. "What's all the arguing about?"

"Dylan says..." started Felicia.

"You always..." said Dylan at the same time.

"Look, you can both invite a friend over if you like. There's enough room in this house for everyone. If you keep on arguing, though, no one is having anyone over."

Felicia ran to the phone to call Mikala. Dylan, meanwhile, had hopped on his bike and headed down to Cooper's house to see if he could spend the night.

Just as dusk began to fall, Dylan and Cooper (with his overnight bag in hand) rode their bikes back to the Drummond's house. Mikala's dad dropped her off. All the kids headed for the kitchen, where Mom had put out some salsa and chips for them to snack on as they waited for pizza to arrive.

"Where's your dad?" asked Cooper bluntly, as they munched chips.

Dylan responded, "He left."

"Left?" said Cooper. "Where did he go?"

"He doesn't live here anymore," muttered Dylan.

Felicia's mom came into the kitchen. "Mr. Drummond and I have been separated for awhile now," she explained to Cooper and Mikala. "We decided it was best for us not to live together anymore."

"Hey, man, I'm sorry," said Cooper to Dylan. "Why didn't you tell me? My mom and dad split when I was about four, but I guess things are okay now."

"You know, my dad who dropped me off here tonight?" said Mikala. "Well, he's my stepdad. My real dad lives in Colorado. I see him in the summers and sometimes on Winter break."

"I didn't know that, Mikala," said Felicia with surprise.

"I don't tell many people," said Mikala. "My stepdad is like my real dad, too. I guess it's kind of neat because I have two dads. Maybe you will have two dads, too, someday."

The doorbell rang and the pizza arrived. Within minutes, the kids forgot all about the conversation and began devouring the pizza. Felicia and Dylan had so much fun that for a little while, they forgot all about Mom and Dad and feeling sad.

My Thoughts

Why do you think Dylan is being mean to Felicia?
How do you think Dylan felt when Cooper asked about his dad?
What do you think Felicia thought about Mikala having a stepdad?
What do you think Felicia and Mikala talked about after dinner?

_____

_____

_____

_____

_____

_____

_____

_____

_____

_____

My Space

Draw or write what you think happened after the pizza arrived.

6

Life Goes On

School passed quickly that year. Felicia had sleepovers with her friends and began to enjoy skating even more than she had before as she got better and better. Dylan began to spend more time at home and began inviting his friends over more frequently.

"You know, Mom," he confided one day. "I used to not like having people over here because I knew you and Dad would get into a fight!"

"It is more peaceful around here now," responded his mom.

Dad continued to organize his new house and enjoy his time with the kids. Mom started getting together with her friends again just like old times. Mom and Dad seemed able to talk to each other now without yelling.

As spring approached, Felicia began to think about her recital. She pulled out the outfit her mom had bought and decided she liked it after all.

When her dad arrived that weekend, she and Mom were planning her recital party. Although she was excited about her recital, she still wished that her dad would just come back home. Life would be so much simpler!

My Thoughts

Why do you think Felicia began to enjoy skating again?
Why did Dylan begin to spend more time at home?
Why do you think Felicia now liked her recital outfit?
How do you think Felicia's Mom and Dad spend their time alone?

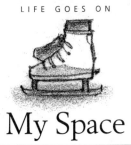

My Space

Draw or write things that kids can do to make themselves feel good.

7

Peace And Love

Finally the day that Felicia had been waiting for was here—the day of her recital. That morning, the telephone rang bright and early. Out of breath from running up the stairs, Felicia answered it.

"Hello?"

"Hi, Sweetpea," said her dad. "I just wanted to tell you how much I love you, and how proud of you...."

"Thanks, Dad," said Felicia, cutting him off. "But I have to run to finish getting ready. Do you want to talk to Mom?"

Felicia felt particularly pretty today. Even Dylan noticed. "Hey, Sis," he said, "that outfit looks pretty cool."

When Felicia, her mom, Dylan, Tyler and Mikala finally made it to the ice arena, Felicia saw her grandma and grandpa standing with her dad. She ran over to them and gave her dad a hug.

"Sweetpea, you look just like a little angel," he said.

"Honey, you look beautiful," said Felicia's grandma.

"You sure do," echoed Grandpa. "What happened to that little girl named Felicia that we used to know? She seems to have disappeared!"

The minute the Drummond family entered the large arena and blended with all the other families, Felicia took off to introduce Mikala to her other friends.

"Hi, Katie," she called to her friend when she saw her down the hall.

"Hi, Felicia," answered Katie. "Are you nervous?"

"I don't think so," said Felicia, "just excited. How about you?"

"Me, too," said Katie. "My brother just flew in, so it's kind of neat to have everybody here."

Soon it was time for the performances to begin. Felicia sat in the front row with her friends waiting to go on stage. She frequently looked back at her family. It was difficult to tell who was beaming the most—Felicia or her family. A feeling of calmness came over Felicia. It was her big day, and the atmosphere felt different somehow. "Everything's really going to be all right," she thought.

After the performances, the announcer thanked the families for coming and he thanked the skaters for trying their hardest. "Remember," he said, "what matters most is that you are a precious gift and that your family loves you very much."

Felicia realized the recital was almost over. It had been a great day. She looked over her shoulder to see if her parents were still sitting next to each other. They were.

Felicia smiled. She knew both her parents loved her very much. And that was enough to make her feel very happy on her special day.

My Thoughts

How do you think Felicia is feeling right now?
How do you think Dylan is feeling now?
Why did Felicia smile when she saw her mom and dad sitting next to each other?
How are you feeling now?

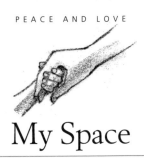

My Space

Draw or write how you see Felicia's family now.

My Space

My Space

My Space

My Space

"Felicia's Family Divorces offers hope and new possibilities through the act of sharing our perceptions of a difficult situation. I appreciate the space for the reader to imagine how they might 'reauthor the story.' I will recommend it to all my patients who are divorcing."

Frances Weintraub, MD,
Pediatrician

"Felicia's Family Divorces is a poignant and accurate portrayal of the roller coast emotions children experience in divorce. Its hopeful lesson is a reassurance that love and support conquer all!"

Donna Roemer, MS,
Guidance Counselor

"I really like the journaling opportunities and questions. This would be an excellent tool for the professional/parent to help children sort through emotions."

Martha York, MSW,
Independent Social Worker

"First, I like the story approach for children. They like stories and I believe that this will encourage children to tell their own stories. There is great value in trying to see things from another person's perspective and in the use of art to display our feelings."

The Rev. Paul Clough,
Presbyterian Church Single Adult
Ministries

"As a teacher, I often have parents come to me and ask for advice on how to help their children deal with a divorce at home. I wouldn't hesitate to offer *Felicia's Family Divorces* as a tool to help them sort through their own feelings as well as help their children do the same."

Kyley Treadwell–Smith,
Elementary School Teacher

"Although designed for use by children, this book offers even greater benefits to parents. I will offer *Felicia's Family Divorces* to my clients in hopes that, by helping the parent gain a greater understanding of everyone's emotional concerns, we can achieve better results for each family without resorting to those difficult courtroom proceedings."

Boyd Farnum, J.D.

"Divorce does not have to be the end. It can be a new beginning. This book will help guide children and influence their parents during this difficult transitional period. Children are always better off with parents who can solve children's issues without court intervention. This book should help parents achieve that goal. I will have copies of *Felicia's Family Divorces* in my lobby and recommend it to all my clients with children."

Dennis Zamplas, J.D.,
Family Law Attorney

"The pain of divorce for young children is well understood but not easily relieved. *Felicia's Family Divorces* provides a useful tool for strengthening a young client's ability to cope with a dark period of life. A welcome addition to the library of any child clinician."

Mark Carpenter, Ph.D.,
Clinical Psychologist

"What a wonderful way to open the door for children to express the uncertainty, anger, sadness and all emotions felt in a divorce. *Felicia's Family Divorces* explains well that these feelings are normal and most importantly that no matter what, they are loved."

Rebecca Nall,
Parent